Return to the Shore

Joe Vigliotti

FutureWord Publishing

© 2010 Joe Vigliotti All Rights Reserved.

ISBN 9780984589029 Return to the Shore

First print August, 2010.

Printed in the United States of America

To God

And every so often
Should the soul, condemned to wander
Retracing footsteps long since faded,
Meet upon the present age
The memories reawakened
Will close one story
And begin another

Chapter One

Winter on the Island is cold and lonely. The winds that whip in from the shore cut across skin like knives. I never went to the shore in the winter when it snowed; photography and painting were nearly impossible then. The wind has a way of racing past you and echoing inside you at the same time. It is as if the wind is making sure you know a void exists within, and the void has yet to be filled. Photography and painting sometimes filled that void, but it never lasted, and I could never paint outside when it snowed.

The water in the summer is a thick gray-green; in the winter, it is mostly gray. The reds and oranges of the trees on the shore in autumn have burned out; everything now is tinted with gray and is dead. It is like the tomb before the Resurrection. There are areas of the shore with sandy beaches that descend gently from the land; there are small and large cliffs that stop suddenly over the choppy water; there are marshes and half-submerged boats still moored to abandoned docks from previous generations, sometimes previous centuries. There are the occasional weathered barns, tired old boathouses, and overgrown farmland in between sprawling estates and carefully-kept property. It is the North Shore.

Every so often, local children or teenagers venturing up from the southern shores happen upon these small pieces of history that the rest of the world forgot in its quest for progress. The little creeks and meandering streams still flow into the ocean. The shadows still remain.

The main points of interest always seem to be the small, forgotten cemeteries around which wood and brush have grown along with superstition and urban legend; tales of ghosts of the early settlers, raving maniacs, and mass murderers captivate entire evenings and provide for sleepless Friday nights. Most of those places are found by accident, having never been intended to be forgotten in the first place, and are rediscovered and remembered. Some are never found again once they have been lost. Some were never meant to be found again.

The faded skull that peered up at me through a pile of leaves and rusted metal seemed out of place, or perhaps, we were. A helicopter circled by overhead with spotlight on. I had received the call about an hour ago; it was nearly two in the morning now. Some teenagers had come to explore a cemetery and had sat down to rest on what appeared to be a small rock outcropping, but there was an old boat against the rocks that gave out beneath their weight. And they found the skull and called.

I wasn't asleep when the station called me. I was painting. I wasn't interrupted though. I had gone as far that night as I could have; I had to wait for the cerulean blue I had used for the sky over a view of Gardiner's Bay to dry before I could put in the trees. Jenson pulled up in front of my house a few minutes later.

And here we stood, near-enough to the shore to hear the ocean when the helicopter was not directly overhead. Jenson lit a cigarette; I don't smoke, and I coughed, and so he took a step to the side and apologized. There were people all around us—some in uniforms, some in shirts and ties like us —and there was the constant flashing of lights and shouting and the occasional bark of search dogs.

And all the time that sad skull peered up at me with hollow eyes. Others were collecting the rest of the bones now. Jenson scratched his head.

"I don't think anyone has been to this part of the Island for years, at least," he said. "What do you think, Gray?" he asked me.

"I don't think so either," I said. "I don't think anyone was supposed to be here again." I knelt down and used a gloved-hand to push away some of the old metal bands that held together the frame of the boat. There were more bones underneath, and the others continued to carefully catalogue and bag them.

"Marcy was slightly unhappy about the call," said Jenson. "It woke the kids up and the baby started crying." He smirked. "I'll have to deal with it when I get home."

"Where are the kids?" I asked one of the officers.

"Over that way," he replied. "I'll take you. They were on their way to an old family cemetery that dates back to the 1600s. The local historical council is already petitioning us to get out of here as soon as possible so they can register the place. Too bad for them it won't happen for a while."

I moved around some more wood. And there, glistening in the flashing light was a small ring. I picked it up and the officer held his flashlight directly over it. I brushed away some dirt and could make out a delicate inscription on the inner side of the band.

"1987," I said out loud to no one in particular.

"Girl?" Jenson asked.

"Probably," agreed one of the officers bagging the remains. "Won't know for sure until we get them to the examiner."

The wind came whipping in from the shore, but I didn't shiver.

Chapter Two

"She was between sixteen and twenty-two," said Roberts, the examiner. I leaned up against a wall in the room and folded my arms. The girl's skeleton was arrayed out on the table like some grotesque piece of modern art; it saddened me that God's handiwork could end up this way. The skull seemed to peer up at me again. Jenson yawned.

"Who was she?" he asked.

"Don't know," mumbled Roberts as he flipped through some pages in a folder. "We're going to do dental work this afternoon and see if we can get an ID as soon as possible."

"Cause of death?"

"Blunt object to the base of the skull," Roberts confirmed as he turned the skull over. "The spine received several blows too, and a few of the ribs were broken."

I had been to countless crime scenes in the seven years I'd been working homicide. The dehumanized nature of what happens dehumanizes you in some ways you wish it didn't, and it hardens you to the world. To do this kind of work, you can't let what you see affect you; and so it hardens you or it consumes you. I hadn't been affected since I'd started. Something this time touched something inside of me. I didn't have words at the time for it.

"How long was she there?" I asked.

"Fifteen, maybe twenty years," Roberts offered. "You can see the decomposition rates if you'd like."

I waved him off. "It's alright," I said. "I trust you."

"You'd better," Roberts boasted. "I've been here thirty years. Haven't been wrong yet." He smugly lifted his coffee mug to his mouth.

"And the ring you found," Roberts added as he looked over at me. "1987."

I nodded.

"It could end up being a graduation ring," said Jenson as he flipped through some papers in another folder. "They're still cleaning it to see if they can find any other inscriptions." Jenson sighed. "It's annoying, isn't it? It's 2008 and we've made so many technological and scientific advances in DNA and behavior and we can't clean a ring fast enough."

Jenson turned around and looked at me. "What were you doing in 1987?"

"I was ten," I replied. "I was proud of Reagan as president and I watched *GI Joe* on television. I wish I could have voted for him."

Jenson grinned. "I voted for Mondale."

"Traitor," Roberts sneered.

"I was young and inexperienced," Jenson simpered before he laughed. Roberts did too. I didn't, but it wasn't because I didn't understand the joke. The emptiness of where the eyes in the skull should be still seemed to bore into me.

The chilly wind that poured through the doorway as we stepped outside seemed to carry away what I felt; or maybe it just quieted the feelings I couldn't put a name to. The numbing of the body that came with the cold always seemed to numb everything else inside of me. A couple, walking by hand-in-hand, didn't bother me as much as it normally would have. They were teenagers. *I wondered if the girl we had found was a teenager;* I thought, *how horrible it must be to have been so young and to be carried away.*

The afternoon shadows were long and lazy across the cold cement. But I thought, *at least she is with Jesus;* the consolation comforted me little. Reason prevents us from seeing clearly sometimes. Maybe it is why we're so cold so often, we refuse to accept the warmth that pervades every moment. But even the most unshakeable will pause occasionally. It's only human, after all.

God knew we would have lapses of judgment, but He knew we could find Him again through Jesus Christ.

Seagulls fluttered overhead and settled on the sidewalk a few feet away from me as Jenson came outside. He lit a cigarette.

"That may kill you one day," I said.

"That's what you think," he argued. "But I've got to smoke while I can. I don't like smoking at home. My kids yell at me more than you do."

I nodded. "See you tomorrow?" I asked.

"Yeah," said Jenson. "Have a good night, Gray. And take it easy."

"You too," I answered. I turned and headed towards the parking lot. The wind swept down from the north now; it was cold, it stung, yet it felt vaguely comfortable. "Get a girlfriend, Gray!" I heard him yell over the wind. "Do something with your night!"

I would do something. I would go home, eat, paint, maybe read a little, watch the news, and go to sleep. It wasn't much, but it sustained me. And it was too cold to paint at the ocean now.

Chapter Three

They ordered us back to the crime scene to do another sweep of the area. They wanted us to establish why the girl had been put there. They wanted us to see if they had missed anything —fragments of clothing, bones, anything. It was normal procedure, but we never found anything. Jenson was driving. He always drove; he didn't like that I rarely went a mile or two above the speed limit.

We made the exit off Sound Avenue towards Asharoken, which sits on a narrow slit of land between Long Island Sound and Northport Bay. Straight down the strip is a small peninsula upon which sits Eaton's Neck, at the end of which is a Coast Guard station. The peninsula is divided in half by a state park. It was towards the west end of the peninsula, east of Pond Drive where they had found her.

The park is heavily-wooded. The trees seem to be endless; each grayed trunk gives way to more behind it. The little cemetery the teenagers were hoping to find was from an early fishing settlement. Over time there have been more than two-hundred shipwrecks there; every so often shifting beach sands reveal the crippled skeletons of boats and the endless waves of time dredge up driftwood. There are also tales of old Indian burial grounds, but they have been lost for now. Every summer, college students try to locate them without success. The remains of an old, lonely lighthouse sit beaten by storm and time; a new lighthouse stands nearby, and the Coast Guard defends and protects, having assumed the burden of centuries past towards new threats to America's shores.

We pulled off the road into a small field. I could hear the ocean; I could feel the wind coming down from the north. Jenson suggested we split up and approach the same place from different directions. I agreed and thought it was only because he didn't want to hear me complain about the cigarettes.

I breathed in deep and began pushing through the woods; the wind caused the branches overhead to creak and sway. There were markers the local police had set up to guide the way to the scene; there was yellow tape around the entire area. As soon as we had gone into the woods, I had lost sight of Jenson. I thought of how lonely the place was. I thought of how far away Eaton's Neck seemed from the rest of Long Island, and I knew then why no one had ever found the girl.

As new little developments continued to encroach upon the park, she would have been found sooner or later. I wondered what the place would be like in the summer, back when the trees were deep shades of green and the forest floor was dotted with shrub and flower and the dry little stream beds were full of water. Over the past few years, as a county investigator, I'd been all over Long Island with the exception of a few places. Eaton's Neck was one of them.

A shrill gust of wind ripped through the trees; my fingertips stung for a moment and I wondered why I hadn't worn gloves as some leaves were kicked up from the ground. Then as suddenly as the wind had come, it had gone; there was silence and cold and the feeling that something was not as it should be.

I kept walking and then stopped. I thought I had heard another set of footsteps; a shifting through dry, cracked winter-weathered leaves, but the footsteps were not there, and I continued. I thought, perhaps, it was Jenson. But the footsteps had seemed to come from another place. And I stopped again, because I thought I heard them again.

I was quiet. There was the far-off sound of the ocean; further away today, it seemed. The wind was high overhead and winding its way through the branches. And then it was as if the entire world was quiet, and to my right there were footsteps; I wasn't hearing things. As I turned around, through the trees emerged the form of a girl. I sighed.

She saw me as she passed through the trees and stopped.

"Oh, hello," she said. "I saw your car out on the road."

"Good afternoon," I said. "You know you're walking through a crime scene."

"Am I?" She sounded surprised. "I didn't know."

"There was yellow tape back around all those trees over there," I pointed back. "You can't be in here."

She looked around her and tightened her crimson scarf; her emerald eyes scanned the land around her and she ran a hand through dark blonde hair.

"I just need to find it," she said. "Then I'll go away and you won't have to worry about me."

"What are you trying to find?" I asked her.

"It's around here, somewhere," she answered. She took a few steps closer to me.

"Every time I come out here, it always seems as if I'm getting lost," she explained. "Would you mind walking around with me for a few minutes? I could use some help."

"This is a crime scene," I insisted. She looked up towards me and raised her eyebrows. I thought perhaps I had been too harsh. "I take it you live nearby?" I asked.

"No," she said. She spun around slowly; her eyes scanned the ground around her. "I was out here the other night, and I lost it, and now I'm looking for it."

"You mean you were out here the other night with that group of kids?" I said.

"Yes," she said as she stepped up in front of me. Her eyes seemed to pierce mine. "My name is Julia Hemdon."

"I'm Detective Gray,"

"Don't you have a first name?" she asked.

"Robert," I acknowledged.

"Well, if you walk around with me for a little while, I'm sure I can find it. And then I'll get out of your way, I promise," she pleaded. She pulled her scarf a little tighter. "I'm cold anyways," she continued. "It would be so much help."

"Alright," I said at last. "But only if you promise to stay away from here after this."

"Thank you," she exclaimed. "I need it for pictures next week."

"Pictures?" I asked as we began to walk.

"Senior portraits. I graduate in a few months."

"Where are you going to go to college?"

"Hopefully here," she said. "But I'm not sure I want to leave."

I nodded. "What are we looking for, by the way?"

"I suppose the best place to look is where I was last," she murmured.

"Where was that?" I asked.

"Oh!" she said. "I just noticed the time. I should probably head back. We have relatives coming over for dinner tonight."

I raised an eyebrow. "A teenager, going home on a Friday night for a family dinner?"

She smiled. "I don't mind. Your family will always be there for you." She smiled again. "Thank you for your help. I hope I didn't bother you."

"No," I reassured. "Not at all. Be safe driving home. Do the speed limit."

"I promise," she replied. "Have a good weekend." She turned around and began to walk towards the road. I turned and began to walk back towards Jenson.

"Maybe I'll see you again!" she called.

I turned around, but she had already disappeared through the trees. I suddenly felt alone when she left. It was as if I suddenly didn't belong there. Odd, I thought. At least she was going home to a family dinner; at least teenagers weren't all bad now. I continued the walk towards Jenson. I couldn't seem to get the girl's face out of my mind; her eyes were bright, and there was something familiar about her. I had probably spoken to her the other night with her friends, the night they found the skeleton.

Jenson was leaning up against a tree near the old boat and rocks, smoking a cigarette. "What took you so long?" he asked. "Get lost?" He smirked.

"Not quite," I said. "I followed the smell of smoke straight to you."

He laughed and I walked over to him. "Believe it or not, I ran into some high school girl."

"Out here?" he quizzed.

"Yeah. She was looking for something she said she had lost out here the other night."

"I didn't see any cars on the road," Jenson remarked. "I guess she must have parked further down."

I nodded in agreement.

Chapter Four

"We're going to shelf the case in another week or two."

I looked up from my desk at Harrison, our department head. I ran a hand through my hair and put down my pen. "Another cold case?" I asked.

"Yep, and twenty years cold at that," he answered. "I'm pulling everyone else off now though except you and Jenson. You can do the research to see if dental records match any missing person's reports, but don't worry about pursuing it too hard. It's going to go nowhere. We may identify the body, but I have no idea how we're going to identify the killer."

"Or killers," I suggested.

Harrison nodded. "Exactly. So don't lose sleep over it. As soon as we get this thing properly catalogued, I'm going to get you and Jenson onto something more recent."

I nodded. Harrison moved around some sketches on the edge of my desk. "I don't know why you never just became an artist," he said.

"The way I want to do art," I said, "doesn't happen now."

"You mean making paintings for a living?"

I nodded. "I would have no source of income."

He nodded and continued looking through the sketches.

"Who is this woman?" he asked. "She's hot." He held up the drawing.

"A sketch of a high school girl I saw at Eaton's Neck yesterday," I answered.

"You didn't hear that," he remarked with a sneer as he put the drawing down. I smirked and he laughed. "Take it easy," he said. "I'll talk to you later."

I pulled the drawing of the girl over to me. I had been up late the previous evening, working especially hard to try to get her eyes just right. There was something different about them. When something bothered me, or affected me, I drew it to try to get it out of my mind. Often it worked; sometimes it didn't.

"Harrison told me to come check out the drawing you'd made of some hot girl," Jenson commented as he stepped up in front of my desk. I handed him the drawing. "She *is* hot."

"She's in high school," I said. Jenson dropped the paper on my desk and walked away quickly as Harrison laughed from somewhere across the room. "Harrison!" he yelled. I grinned.

I looked at the drawing again. There was something about her eyes. They were bright, but they were sad. I closed my eyes, and I searched for hers, thinking that perhaps I had drawn them incorrectly. Her eyes were there, and they were bright but sad, just like my drawing. *Why are you sad*, I thought. A family, a future, kindness… and sadness.

~

A few days later, Jenson came back and set a folder on my desk. "They finished cleaning the ring," he said. "Have a look." I opened the folder; he continued as I flipped through a few photographs. "It's from Westview High School, south near Babylon. The initials on the ring looked like they were either accidentally or purposely scraped off, so that doesn't help us any. But we know where to look now for missing persons reports and where to search for dental records."

I looked at the photos. There was a lacrosse stick on one side; there was a cross on the other. It sent a chill down my back. I wondered how many teenagers would have the courage or the faith to do that, especially now. I closed the folder and said a silent prayer.

Chapter Five

I was replacing the yellow tape when Julia walked up behind me. Some local teenagers had torn it all down and wrapped it around someone's car on the other side of the park. I had come out to do another sweep of the area; I was afraid that we would suspend the case and something would turn up which I had overlooked, or that the area would simply be paved over and something that could have turned up would be forever lost. I kept thinking of how things had turned out with Green River.

"You're still here?" she asked as I turned around.

"I should say the same thing about you,"

She smiled. "I thought I would see you again."

"What are you doing here?"

"I still haven't found it." Her smile disappeared. "I know it's here."

"Did you have anything to do with tearing down this tape?"

"No," she objected. "I wouldn't do that to you. I've been back a few times and it's always so lonely here. But I'm glad you're here now, because now it's not lonely. Will you be here long?"

"Probably,"

"Good," she said. "That gives us lots of time to look and to talk."

"To talk? You really shouldn't be here. It's a crime scene."

"I'm not afraid of it," she assured. "And besides, you're here, so that's all the more reason not to be afraid. And it's funny, because I've been so afraid lately."
She spoke with such sadness in her voice that I suddenly felt bad for trying to make her go away.

"Well let's have a look," I said at last, hoping that I didn't sound condescending.

"Thank you," she murmured softly. "Well you were here alone, and I was here alone, but now we're not alone." She smiled. "Why were you out here by yourself?"

"I was going to do another search and see if there was something I could find that I couldn't find before."

"You and me both," she consented quietly. "I always seem to find you though. Two times now. I'm almost positive God intended it."

I nodded. "You're probably right. But what reason could there possibly be?"

"Does it matter? We'll find out; sooner or later we will. We just have to trust Him."

We walked in silence for a moment. I could hear the ocean, and the wind. Julia's eyes scanned the ground methodically.

"It's hard to find things sometimes," she explained.

"What are you going to do in college?" I asked.

"Probably political science," she said. "I'd like to get involved and change things."

"What would you change?" I pressed.

"People," she replied. "As much as it was possible to do. People say that chivalry is dead, but it isn't. I would work for a better culture, a better way of living. For common decency, maybe. For respect."

I smiled. "I take it you're quite traditional?"

"Oh yes," she responded. "I am. Much more so than most of my friends. It makes for interesting conversations because they have varying ideas about those kinds of things."

"That's how my friends are," I explained.

"Everyone understands things differently. What matters is the answer." She paused a moment, and then looked at me. "Why did you decide to become a detective?"

"I wanted to help people," I said. "This seemed the most immediate way."

She smiled. "Not many people are that thoughtful anymore."

"I suppose. Not many teenagers would come out and say they're traditional either."

"I'm not afraid to stand up for what I believe in," she asserted.

"Not very many people are that way anymore," I mused.

"I know," she said. She climbed up onto a log and began to walk along it as I walked along on the ground beside her, and she put her hand on my shoulder to steady herself every so often; when she got to the end of the log she sat down.

"It's nice out here, isn't it?" she remarked. She put her hands beneath her legs on the log and snuggled into her scarf and coat. "And a little cold," she added.

"I think maybe you'd better head back," I suggested.

"I'm not cold enough yet," she objected. "And besides, if I don't find it, I don't want to."

"You can always come back on a warmer day," I suggested optimistically.

I raised an eyebrow. She smiled at me. "Why not bring some of your friends to help?" I asked.

"Too annoying, they wouldn't have the patience for it." She looked around.

"And besides," she added, "I feel safe with you."

I wasn't quite sure how to answer. She responded for me. "I am getting a little cold. Let's go walk to the shore, and then I'll leave. I promise."

I nodded; she smiled and stood up. She walked beside me; her hair swirled around in the wind. She spoke about how her grandfather had been a fisherman, and how he still fished off Fire Island recreationally. She spoke about how some of her uncles were still fishing, and how they lived at the northeastern end of the Island. She spoke about how her sister was a teacher in North Babylon. We crossed the road and continued off into a small field and another patch of woods. The sounds of waves grew louder.

At last we came to the shore. The waves were never large on the north side of the Island. It was, after all, a bay. We wandered over to the water's edge. The sand over which we crossed was hardened from frost that morning. Far out on the water there were a few fishing boats. A brave mariner had taken out his speedboat. The wind whipped in, harsh and cold.

"On clear days, you can see Connecticut," she commented as she wrapped her arms around her slender frame.

"I know," I said.

She turned to me and smiled.

"I'm glad I met you." Julia turned back towards the ocean.

"I'm glad I met you, too," I replied.

It was too cold for painting, I thought. I rarely ever came to the shore in the winter because of that. I looked off towards where Connecticut would be, and I looked off northeast towards the vast openness of the Atlantic. I wondered; if I left, if I kept going, if I never came back, if I was able to, if it was possible to, could I keep going? Would forever always last?

Julia inched closer to me and our arms touched. I could feel her shivering. I wondered what she was thinking; I wondered if she'd thought what I'd thought. Maybe she was shivering from the cold; maybe there was something else. It was as unknown to me as forever.

"I'm cold," I lied. "Maybe we should go?"

"Alright," she agreed. "I'm cold too."

And we turned and treaded back up towards the woods and the field. And when we got to the road, she stopped, and said, "My car is up this way. Yours is down there. I hope I see you again." She looked sad.

"If God intended it," I said, "we will." She smiled, and she hugged me, and she turned around and seemed to glide away. She left me standing there, questioning myself and my place in God's plan. I thought I had figured out my role. The girl had changed everything I knew.

Chapter Six

"Strike!" shouted Jenson.

"Too bad we're not playing baseball," said Harrison. "You'd be in serious trouble."

"Be quiet," Jenson smugly replied. "That's only because you're losing . . . again!"

"Shut up Jenson," jeered Harrison as he picked up a ball. "Or I'll put you in filing for the next five years."

I smirked and leaned back in my chair. Roberts had come with us tonight, and he was finishing his burger. Every weekend, we always did something. During the summer months, we would go fishing or out on Harrison's boat in the evenings with everyone's kids. During the winter, we usually bowled. The collision of pin and ball sent loud echoes bounding off the wooden floors.

The building we were in was converted into a bowling alley from an old World War II munitions warehouse. Much the way that crumbling old farmhouses were reclaimed by the land, so too were elements of history by human nature. Long Island had certainly seen its own share of history. Every time I went into the city, I was always captivated by random markers talking about the evacuation and battle during the Revolution; except for those markers, the event might never have happened: the old battlefield is a sprawling array of entrance and exit ramps and apartment buildings. It seems that progress forgets its past sometimes.

"Strike!" yelled Jenson.

"Filing!" Harrison yelled back..

"You yell more than teenagers!" said Jenson's wife, Marcy. Harrison's wife, Hannah, nodded. Their kids had their own lane next to ours. Roberts's wife Ellen was over ordering the kids food.

"Obviously you've never been around teenagers," rebuffed Jenson. "You should hear the way they yell when we have to arrest them."

"That's why I work in an office," said Roberts. "I do real work."

"If you consider napping at your desk all day 'real work,' that's alright," said Harrison.

"Hey, Harrison," said Roberts. "How would you like to make this interesting?"

"Are you speaking of a wager, my friend?" said Harrison with a grin as he crossed his arms.

"I am indeed," said Roberts. "Fifty dollars."

"Very well," agreed Harrison.

"I'm in too," added Jenson.

"No," was the simultaneous reply from both Roberts and Harrison. Harrison explained: "We're making a wager, not being stupid."

"Look, just because I happen to be winning this round …" Jenson stretched his arms.

"You win every round," said Roberts. I smirked. Jenson did always win. I don't ever recall him not winning.

There was some cheering to the side, and I looked over at a group of young men. They were Marines. They were laughing and getting their things together. Harrison said, "Hey, Jenson! Why don't you go challenge those kids?"

"Can't," said Jenson as he grinned.

I looked back over at the Marines. They were a part of a unit that had recently returned from a successful tour in Iraq. As they passed by us, a few of them stopped.

"You again!" one of them said.

"What?" said Jenson.

"I don't want to see you ever again," the Marine laughed.

Jenson looked at us and grinned.

"Jenson!" said Roberts. "Why not challenge these young men to a game?"

"With all due respect sir," said the Marine, "facing down a terrorist is one thing, but facing down this man is something else." He pointed to Jenson. "I lost fifty bucks last weekend." His buddies laughed with him.

Chapter Seven

I couldn't sleep that night, so I went and stood in the back-yard. The only lights on were streetlamps up and down the road. There wasn't a lot of wind, but the trees at the corner of my yard still swayed back and forth. I walked over towards them and leaned up against one. I looked upward to the sky; the moon was hidden behind low gray clouds.

I closed my eyes, and I saw Julia's face. There was something unmistakably sad about her; I could see it in her eyes. Normally when kids come into the station and something is wrong, you can simply sense it. The sadness from this girl was overwhelming. It was why I didn't just order her away from the scene like I had with other kids before. It was why I hadn't minded speaking with her. There was something so different about her, and it wasn't her faith or her beliefs.

I thought about the things she had said; I thought about the way she had put her hand on my shoulder; I thought about the hug she had given me before turning away to go home. There should have been no reason for her to touch me, but she had; maybe she was lonely.

The wind picked up a little, and I heard it sail through the branches. I kept my eyes closed and remembered how it would sound in the summer, when the tree was full of leaves and the world was alive.

I thought of the shore at summer, too. I thought of the afternoons and the evenings I'd spent painting, and reading, and trying to find something other than the yellow tape that kept my mind confined to the crimes. In the summer, the world was full of color: of deep greens and autumn-colored sunsets and pastel flowers; the winters were variations of gray, and kept me trapped and focused on those yellow boundaries.

I'd almost quit a few times when I started; I'd almost decided to find something else to do. But I couldn't seem to get away from it; I knew of guys who had burned out quickly, and then I knew of guys like Harrison and Roberts that had been in it forever.

Days like yesterday, when I stood on the shore with Julia, when the ocean seemed to beckon me out and away, I wondered if I shouldn't be doing something else. I wondered what it would be like to touch forever. I wondered how long the sea had tempted man to cross it; to find out what was on the other side; to find what awaited. The ocean that I really stood at existed somewhere inside of me.

Her eyes had changed something inside of me. God knew what; I didn't. God knew why, and I didn't.

God was like and unlike the ocean. He made us wonder; He made us question and try to answer. But no matter how we tried, we could never cross that metaphysical ocean that separated us. He came to us in His own time.

What is it, I wondered, *What have You planned for me? What has changed?*

I sat down with my back against the tree. I thought of the girl under the boat. It wouldn't be long before they figured out who she was. I wondered what she wanted to do with her life. I wondered how her loss affected God's great plan. There was so much that we could never know while we were here in this place. Hard times do one of two things: they drive you closer to the Truth, or further away from it.

I had found my father when I was eight; he was face-down on the steps with a knife in his back. It was the miserable outcome of a petty mugging. He was a policeman. My mother moved us out of the city to Long Island after that.

She died a few years later; my brother died on September 11th. He was a firefighter.

For a while, I was driven away from the Truth; for a while, I couldn't recognize it. I wondered: how beautifully, tragically ironic that Pilate should ask "what is truth?" without recognizing that Truth stood before him. And I drifted the other way: sooner or later, truths were always revealed.

The moon peered out from behind the clouds and cast a gentle blue light over everything. It was as if the world was luminescent, and I found myself drawn closer than before. I could feel God's presence: I had this feeling, this innate idea that everything was right; that everything was as it should be. His plan was proceeding as He intended it to. His will is executed through His creation.

I saw Julia's face again, It was uncertain—and the sadness was ever present. It was as if she was waiting for something. But waiting for what?

Chapter Eight

It was another sleepless night. I didn't have to go in Saturday, so I decided to drive up the coast to Eaton's Neck. There was something ethereal about the great expanse of unused land there; something strange and silent and separate from the rest of the world. There was no traffic, there were no robberies, there was no congestion and noise and hectic movement and there was no nightmarishly-quick pace to life. Little pieces of the past always turned up there, tucked away and forgotten in quiet corners that were only waiting to be taken.

The sun was out today. I parked on the side of the road and I decided to walk over to the shore where Julia and I had traversed earlier. It seemed as if time had stopped, and it seemed like it had been years since we had walked to the water. I was tired, but I couldn't sleep, and I wouldn't take medication to fall asleep. I didn't drink coffee to stay awake either.

I never drank either. I took a general philosophy course as a way to fill up credit in college; I ended up falling in love with it and minored in the subject. Kant was one of those masterful minds that appealed to me deeply. Kant was concerned with absolute values and absolute morals. He saw any surrendering of our rational free will as a crime against ourselves; it was all the more reason I didn't drink: I couldn't stand not being in control of myself. Colds were worse enough without voluntarily resigning my capacity for clear judgment to alcohol's discretion.

Murders infuriated me. It was the intentional destruction of human life, the total destruction of free will and of choices. You were denying another human being of the right to exist.

Arms found their way around me in a hug. It was Julia. She smiled, as she always did, and stepped up beside me.

"How do you always manage to find me?" I asked.

"Maybe it's that *you* found *me*," she answered.

"Maybe."

"What are you doing out here?" she asked.

"I'm not sure, really," I replied. "I felt like coming."

"Me too," she said.

"Are you still looking?" I asked.

"Yes," she admitted. "But I know I'll find it."

The thoughts seemed to fall into place; I thought she must be looking for the cemetery, for some old landmark. She would stumble across it sooner or later, I thought. That is, unless the historical society built a wall around it.

"Did you ever stop to wonder about what it is you're doing?" she asked.

I looked over at her. The sun was setting, and I could see the horizon in her eyes.

"Yes," I said.

"I have too," she said. "I'm eighteen, and every time I think I've figured something out, it opens up far more than I want to know or think about could happen. You wonder if everything you're doing is right."

"What are you doing?" I asked.

"I'm not sure. I'm never very sure now."

"Why is that?"

"With school over soon, and with college . . . I'm just not sure . . ."

"Not sure of what you're going to do after college?"

"Yeah," she answered. She looked up at me. "Don't get me wrong," she continued. "There are a lot of things I want to do. I'm just not sure what's going to happen."

"Only a few people ever know this early on what it is they want to do with their lives," I said. "And as long as you're doing something, you're set. Some people take a lifetime."

She nodded. "I just want to make sure that I do something. That I'm not intended for nothing."

She was so sad, and she wrapped her arms around herself.

"You're not intended for nothing," I said. "Life isn't certain. But the one thing we can be certain of is that God has a plan for everyone. We're not meant to be here for nothing."

"I hope so," she agreed.

"Do you remember the other day when you said that perhaps God intended us to meet?"

"I do," she replied. Her eyebrows lifted a little and her eyes widened.

"Well, if He had intended something as simple as our meeting, how could He not have intended anything greater for you?"

She was quiet for a moment. I could see a flash of sunlight in her eyes and the interminable breadth of existence.

"And besides," I said, "from what I know of you, I don't see how God couldn't have intended anything for you. You're meant for something."

She looked up at me, eyes full of searching and uncertainty.

"I'm just scared to leave, I suppose," she murmured..

"I thought you wanted to go to school locally?" I reminded her.

"Yes," she admitted as her eyes drifted towards mine. "I'm just afraid to leave now."

I nodded. I knew what she meant. I looked at her footprints in the sand beside mine.

She handed me a slip of paper. "It's my phone number," she explained. "I feel like I've known you longer. Promise me that no matter where we end up, even if I don't see you here again, that you won't let me go."

"Not at all," I said. I handed her one of my cards. I put her paper in my coat.

"That way if I forget, you won't," I explained.

"I'll be back," she said. "We're going away for Easter. But I'll be back here again right after that. I hope you will too."

She hugged me, and left me standing there. But she smiled when she left this time. I hoped it was a genuine smile.

Chapter Nine

"Her name is Julia Hemdon."

My heart stopped; nothing else in the world moved. I couldn't breathe. I thought there must be some mistake.

"Her name is Julia Hemdon."

The folder lay open on my desk; an enlarged copy of the girl's high school portrait stared me in the face: the emerald-green eyes, the smile, the long dark blonde hair draped around her shoulders.

"She was eighteen . . ."

She had hugged me. I had seen her so many times. It must have been a different girl; a relative; the same name, different girl; it couldn't be her.

". . . Reported missing one evening after going out with a group of friends . . ."

I had just seen her. She was alive. She had hugged me. I had spoken to her less than a week ago. I had seen her footprints in the sand beside mine.

". . . was going to major in political science . . ."

It was impossible. My heart was being ripped into a thousand pieces; there was disbelief, there was denial, there was even some heartache. The girl was alive. I still couldn't look at the photo of the skeleton. I kept her portrait over it.

"Are you alright, Gray?"

I looked up. "Yeah," I said quickly. "I haven't been feeling too well lately. Stomach virus," I lied.

"Well take it easy man. We're going to wrap this case up soon enough."

"Alright," I said to Harrison.

I did become physically ill. Harrison sent me home early, but I didn't go home: I drove out to Eaton's Neck. I parked, and I leapt out of the car, and I sprinted over to the woods.

"Julia!" I yelled.

"Julia! I'm here!"

I ran over to where the boat had been, to the spot where we had found the body, but I couldn't look. I called for her.

I thought perhaps maybe she was down the road; I ran down the narrow lane as fast as my legs could carry me. The wind tore into my skin like a thousand knives, and my coat unfurled madly behind me, and my hair was across my eyes. I was looking for her car, for any sign at all that she was there, that she had been there. But there was nothing.

And I ran to the beach even faster. I tripped across the sand beyond the little meadow and I cut my hand and I picked myself up and kept running. I could see the water.

"Julia!" I called.

I already knew she wouldn't be there, but I had to prove it to myself that she wouldn't answer, that she wouldn't be standing there. Something was wrong, something had happened. I wasn't crazy; I knew she was there. I knew what I had seen; I knew what I had felt.

I got to the edge of the water and I collapsed onto my knees. What had happened to me, I wondered. Had I imagined everything? I couldn't have. How had I seen her? Nothing made sense.

Chapter Ten

There was still a part of me that didn't want to believe; there was a part of me that couldn't believe. There was an emptiness I felt. It was a loss I had not felt the presence of for what seemed years since I had met her.

I had dinner the evening before Easter with Jenson's family. I hadn't gone to Christmas dinner, and so they had obligated me for Easter.

It was warm. We were out back and Jenson's kids were on the swings while he smoked. His daughter yelled at him to stop. Jenson put out the cigarette and said, "I hope you harass your mother about the amount of time she takes at the store."

"I heard that!" came Marcy's voice from inside. Jenson laughed, and we moved away from the door.

"I still don't believe you," he said "I wouldn't believe it if I were you."

"I'm not sure I do believe it," I confessed. "But the girl was there, no doubt about it."

"Okay," offered Jenson. "She probably was there, but it probably was a different Julia Hemdon. Or maybe it was some girl with a similar-sounding name. Or maybe it was some girl playing a prank on you. Or maybe-"

"Or maybe it was her ghost," I suggested "Or maybe her spirit."

Jenson raised an eyebrow. "I saw the drawing earlier. The girls do look the same—between your sketch and the photo, they look the same, I mean. But isn't it possible that maybe you remembered wrong or the girl is a relative or?"

"She was real," I insisted. "She was real."

Jenson crossed his arms. "And you have the paper she wrote on."

"Yes," I answered as I unfolded it from my pocket carefully. Jenson glanced at it again and shook his head.

"So Julia Hemdon's ghost has a thing for you." He grinned. I shook my head.

"I don't know what to do," I said.

"Well, just don't follow her off a ledge or something," said Jenson. "Just because she's a ghost and can fly doesn't mean you can."

"You've been watching too much television," I said. "And I saw that show too. But the only flaw is that I don't live in a high rise."

"Well don't ever live in one," said Jenson. "I don't want to come by to get you one day and have you land on top of me."

"At least you'd break my fall," I smugly replied.

"I'll make sure I'm smoking at the time," he leered. "Then maybe I'll burn you on the way out."

"Thanks."

"Don't mention it."

"I still don't know what to do," I said.

"If you really are seeing her ghost," said Jenson, "and your story is true, I'd just head back up there again and see what there is to see. Why not? It's not like you have a busy schedule. You're lucky we're cousins."

I smirked. "Right."

"I suppose," said Jenson, "that if this is the case, I would just let things keep going. God must have a hand in it somehow."

"I thought so too, perhaps," I said.

"He'd better have a hand in this or I'm going to end up thinking you're crazy," Jenson joked.

"You wouldn't be alone. I think I'm crazy too," I said.

"You're not crazy," he reassured. "You know I was only joking."

"I know," I said; "I just wish I knew that I wasn't crazy."

"I think she's right," Jenson said.

"What do you mean?" I asked.

"There's a reason for it. There's a reason for everything. You taught me that a long time ago."

"If only I could make myself believe it," I said.

"It takes time."

"I know."

"Too bad, isn't it?"

"Time never goes quickly unless you don't want it to. And then you wake up, and it's gone before you realize you can't stop it."

Jenson nodded.

"You remember when grandpa died?"

"Yeah."

"Right before he died, he told me that everything happens for a reason. He's the one who taught it to me," I said. "He was smarter than he ever gave himself credit for."

Jenson nodded. "Maybe you are too."

"Maybe I'm crazy."

Marcy opened the door to the deck and said, "Get the kids to come in because it's time for dinner. That includes both of you."

Joe Vigliotti

Chapter Eleven

On Monday morning I opened up the old files. Harrison hadn't told us to shut down yet, and so I kept looking. They were in the process of digitizing all our written records, but they hadn't gotten very far yet. I also pulled all the most recent ones we had.

I was disappointed, but I wasn't surprised that there was so little they had on the case. Julia was killed back in the eighties, back before the housing expansion that started in 1990. There had been almost no one living out towards that part of Eaton's Neck yet.

The folders were old and the edges were wrinkled and faded; they were covered with dust when I pulled them out. I set them out on my desk and I turned each page carefully, hoping that I wouldn't miss anything someone else had. Time managed to forget most things; I didn't want to be a part of time.

There were written statements from the few people that could be rounded up; new interviews said there was nothing out of the ordinary, they all said in one way or another. They hadn't noticed anything, if they could remember back that far. The missing person's report about Julia didn't yield anything either; I was as without direction as when I began. I closed my eyes; how I wanted to see her again. I still couldn't believe it was real; the paper in my pocket was proof enough though. It was proof I couldn't accept wholeheartedly.

The old missing-persons folders were empty of anything useful; the new folders added nothing. I kept Julia's yearbook photo over the autopsy photos. I couldn't stand to see them.

Julia didn't come back to the beach Monday. I was there for a few hours; it wasn't as though I had anything else to do in the evenings anyway. She had said after Easter; she had never said how long after.

I watched a few boats heading back towards harbor; there were some fishing vessels and some smaller boats. And then I looked up.

The boat.

I was back across the little field and the road and into the woods as fast as I could be. I ducked the yellow tape as I ran and came to a short stop just before the old boat. I knelt down and I sifted through the pieces of wood that had been laid out. There were chips of white paint on some of the pieces; others were completely weather-worn. The investigative team hadn't removed the entire thing.

I finally found what I was looking for on the other side of the hull, on the side that had been nestled against the rocks—a name.

Chronos.

As I went to stand up I tripped on some of the metal bands and almost cut my face across one. As I opened my eyes I noticed on the inside of one of the bands a few long, jagged scratch marks.

Julia's ring. She wasn't dead when they left her.

I wasn't sure when I would be able to breathe again.

Chapter Twelve

I pulled all the files I could on robberies in the area the next morning. None of them had been digitized. They were the last files scheduled to be scanned. I narrowed down theft to maritime vessels, and then to smaller boats. I had about a hundred different incidents to go over. I explained to Harrison what I was doing when he asked and then he shrugged and went to get coffee.

After a phone call I drove up past Asharoken to Eaton's Neck an hour later with an address. I ended up at the southwest corner of the land and I could see back across to the Island and the tiny strip of land where Asharoken sat.

I was shown around to the back of a rather large home by a landscaper to where George Tharsley was raking. He shook my hand and his wife offered me a drink which I declined.

"1987," said Tharsley. "I can't believe someone would be calling me back all this time about that boat, and especially not under these circumstances."

"They're regrettable," I agreed. "But anything you can tell me would be of tremendous help."

"Of course," said Tharsley. He pointed out towards the edge of his property, towards a boathouse and a long wooden dock. We walked out onto it over the water and he gestured with his hand out across the waves.

"There was a storm, well-near a hurricane we got hit with that spring," he said. "They evacuated the Neck. When I came back, the boat was gone and I thought the storm had swept it away; I had it tied up on the shore over there," he said as he pointed to where the grass met the ocean.

"And then when I went to go see if it had maybe ended up somewhere further down the shore, I noticed that the ropes I had used to tie it down were still there. I looked them over and found out they had been cut, not frayed like it had snapped. So I called you guys, and an officer confirmed it had been cut."

"And there were never any leads?" I asked.

"No, unfortunately," said Tharsley. "If I hadn't built that boat myself, I wouldn't have said anything about it. I can buy a new boat, easily; building one is personal though. And then I had the boathouse built not long after it."

I nodded.

"Although . . . "

I looked over at Tharsley. He put a finger to his chin and furrowed his eyebrows. "I do remember thinking it might have been some kids, but I couldn't have been sure."

"What makes you think that?"

"Well, I'm sure you know all about the groups of tee-nagers that come up here all the time looking for ghosts and everything. I did it too when I was a kid. But I remember a group wandering onto my property a few days before the evacuation. They might have just gotten lost; most of the Neck was wooded back then. They showed up again two days later and I yelled at them that they were on my property. I don't mind when kids end up here on accident; when they show up more than once —and they're the same group of kids more than once—then I start wondering. If they say hello and want to talk, I don't mind; these kids just had this look that they were up to something.

"That's about all I do remember though," he said.

"Thank you," I replied. "You've been a big help."

"You're welcome, sir," he said. "And, oh, before I forget—my next door neighbor over there"—he pointed again—"Henry Grier—he mentioned something to me about a group of kids cutting across his property right before the storm. You could go talk to him; he might be of more help."

I said thank you, and Tharsley called ahead to let Grier know I was coming.

Grier's wife greeted me at the door and led me into an expansive living room where Grier was online. He was much older than Tharsley, and he greeted me with a smile and a handshake. He maneuvered his way with a cane to large glass doors at the back of the room; he was a veteran.

"Yeah, I saw those kids," said Grier. "The same group cut across my property a few times. That's unusual. George and I think they had something to do with the theft of his boat."

"And they were the exact same kids each time?" I asked.

"Almost," said Grier. "There were four guys and a girl that I recognized the second and third time. I think they must have been athletes because they were wearing school colors and hooded sweatshirts. But once they had a new girl with them. It was the only time I'd seen her."

Julia, I thought silently.

"And then I never saw them after that day. I was leaving and I saw a blue pickup truck parked on Pond Drive over there, past the houses. I figured it was theirs. I'm sorry I can't be of more help," he said regretfully. He also mentioned the school colors.

"That's quite alright," I replied. "You and Mr. Tharsley have been a greater help than you know."

Chapter Thirteen

Wednesday afternoon I found Julia again. She claimed, like normal, that she had found me. It was warmer that day; a few seagulls wandered around the beach. She felt real. I hugged her and she hugged me more tightly than I could remember her doing before.

"I missed you," she said.

"I missed you too,"

"Are you alright?" she asked. "You look a little pale." She put her hand up to my face and touched my cheek, and I jumped a little. Seeing her for the first time now that I knew what had happened made everything seem so much more surreal. Her hand was warm and she seemed so alive.

"I am," I lied. I shivered, and so she hugged me again. She was warm, she was alive; she was dead, but who were we to say what was real and not? Only God knows those kinds of things. God is real.

I suddenly wondered when the last time I had been to Church was.

"I'm here now," she said. "You have nothing to worry about."

I breathed in deeply. Half of me wanted to wrap my arms around her and protect her with the thought that I had nothing to fear; half of me knew that it was already too late and I still wanted to hold onto her and protect her.

I wondered if she knew she was dead.

"I was alone again," she said. "I had a wonderful time over Easter, but I'm glad to be back home. And I'm not alone now."

"Never," I whispered.

She heard me. She smiled.

"How did you know I was worried?"

"I can tell," she continued. "Before you ask, I just can."

The answer settled the issue. My mind began to wander. I had read before the theories of ghosts, about residual and active hauntings and I wondered how I fit into her world. I wondered if she had somehow crossed the threshold of time; Saint Augustine was convinced time did not exist; Einstein believed the past and the present and the future ran parallel together. Perhaps those boundaries bled into one another somewhere, somehow. Only God knows.
God is time.

I looked at Julia. The sinking sun to the west glittered off the water as it hadn't done since the fall and she seemed to light up in the gentle orange glow; she looked out across the water and it was as if time stood still. For a moment, there was only the two of us on that sandy ground, standing somewhere, somehow; there was nothing more but there was nothing less, and there was the promise of something else. But what else could there be? Did God want me to find an answer to this moment amid an infinite method of mystery?

"I feel safe with you," she sighed.

We parted ways after the sun had drifted into the west, but the light was still in her eyes.

Chapter Fourteen

Harrison shrugged his shoulders. "I hope you know what you're doing, because I sure don't." He took a sip of his coffee. "I'll come back in a while to see if you're still alive. I suppose we should really digitize all of this, shouldn't we?"

I had several stacks of folders across my desk. "Maybe," I said. "But that takes the fun out of this. Want to help?"

"I have to go check to make sure the coffee machine is still working," Harrison grinned.

I had remembered what Grier had said about the blue pickup and specific school colors. I had combed through school websites and identified a handful of schools with the same colors, and from those districts I went through auto records to track down families that had purchased blue pickups from the late seventies and on to 1987. I came up with almost two-hundred possibilities.

I had to sort through each one and take it case-by-case. I prayed that I was doing something right. There was, after all, the chance that someone sold the truck to someone else and was untraceable or something of the sort. There had to be an end.

I developed a system. I ruled out trucks sold out-of-state and trucks destroyed in accidents. They wouldn't have been of use in 1987 if they had been put out of use before then. That cut the number down by about twenty; not much help in the end, but still some.

I kept Julia's photo propped up against a stack of folders as I continued to sift through papers; her sad eyes seemed to watch over me, and I felt as though I was headed in the right direction. Her eyes were unlike the eyes I saw myself; the eyes I had seen were alive, and alight with life. I couldn't stand to look at the autopsy photographs; I hadn't looked at them since the beginning. I wanted to believe I'd never look at them again.

The eyes from the photograph continued to look out at me, or so I liked to think. They were eyes that were sad and uncertain, but they had the world in them. There was so much in her eyes; they had changed me, somehow; they had changed something inside of me.

Whoever had silenced those eyes would have to answer for it sooner or later; I hoped it was sooner, and I hoped that it would be at my hands.

I had finally settled on two blue pickup trucks in Julia's school district. Each story had to work. All the others I had eliminated for one reason or for another; the timing was imperfect, the method inadequate.

Both pickups were still retained by the original owners; both pickups were the same model; the owners of both pickups had had children in high school in 1987.

I explained what I was doing to Harrison that day; he thought perhaps I was going too far: after all, what were the chances? It was all circumstantial evidence; no amount of circumstantial evidence would hold up in court for a case this old and the participants so long removed. There was no DNA.

The most I could do was to place a blue pickup at the scene of the crime with Julia; in fact, other than my own belief, I couldn't even place her with that group of kids. What was I hoping to accomplish, Harrison wanted to know; what was it that I wanted to do; why was it that he shouldn't shut me down immediately and put me on something else?

I could have tried the explanation, the truth; but Harrison wasn't my cousin like Jenson; maybe I should have explained that I was talking to some murdered girl's ghost, that I wanted to find her killer to exact, at the worst, some kind of revenge and at best, simply living content with the knowledge alone that I knew who had killed her; I could imagine him asking me to take some time off. I settled for the most comprehensive, revealing explanation without lying:

"I just want to make sure I don't miss anything before it's too late."

Harrison nodded. "Don't kill yourself over it," he said; "It's good you're doing something, maybe. It's slow now. Things always pick up in the summer; you know how the seasons operate. So get whatever it is you need to get done finished. Summer is just around the corner."

I combed through old yearbooks at the library and came across Julia's photo, and I came across the photos of the two high school students whose parents owned blue pickups. Both had the look of confidence; both were athletes; one played football, one wrestled. But from there, I had nothing to go on. Anything after that, I would have to dig deeper or attempt to illicit something from Julia. But how was I to manage that?

Chapter Fifteen

I wondered how often people were in contact with the dead. I wondered how it was possible. I had often heard that the dead are fated to dwell in this world before rejoining God until their spirits can be put at rest; they had unfinished business. Julia had unfinished business. She was looking for her killer; it was what she was looking for: the solution to her unfinished business. I thought perhaps that if I could determine who it was, I could show her, and she could go see God at last, that her questions would be answered. The longer it took me, the longer it took her; she deserved so much better that what had happened to her. I wanted to protect her. I was doing the best I could now.

My dreams were a torrent of wonder: of darkness, of God's presence in the darkness, of being somewhere without recognizing where it was that I stood. There were stars, and I was on the shore, but this was a shore I had never seen before. There were meadows and fields and woods and the beach and the water, but there was nothing else.

The waves swept away from shore, not towards it; each wave pulsated with a soft, luminescent blue light that raced out through the shore like lightning through a storm-swept sky, but without the storm. There was a wind that came towards me, and fell away and fell down and went up. I knelt down before the water and I touched it. A spiral of light emanated from where I had touched.

This was a place and a darkness that was unlike any other; there was no fear, just peace. Each light that echoed up from the water was peace.

And then the wind swept around behind me and raced through the summer trees; and the trees, like guides, seemed to beckon towards the vast heavens— great lights that seemed to come from the horizon. There was a whirl-wind of lights that chorused up from the trees and ascended through the dark firmament an opening in the darkness, a pure sky blue glow. And as I watched the lights chorus around me, I noticed that it was not a continuous stream of light. It was intermittent, and it was ultimately not light at all: each intermittent streak was the shape of a person, their legs blurred by motion and their arms outstretched towards Heaven. And I wondered: *Where was I?*

And from beside me I felt a great warmth; there was a hand on my shoulder and I turned and found Julia, and she smiled and it seemed as though every pain in her was gone. She looked at me and she pointed towards the sky; she couldn't go yet, and it was because of me that she couldn't go. But there was no anger towards me because of it; she smiled, and her eyes told me that she trusted me, that she knew I would not abandon her.

She knew.

Chapter Sixteen

She was reading at the shore when I found her. Her crimson scarf was tucked into her jacket, and she was sitting with her legs crossed. I stepped up beside her, and she looked up at me with the saddest eyes I had ever seen.

"So you know," she said.

I didn't say anything; I sat down beside her.

"The other day, right after Easter, I knew you already knew," she said. "But I wanted to make sure, and so I visited you last night. I wanted to tell you in a way I know wouldn't hurt you as much, and I took you to the place where everyone leaves this world."

"So that place is real?" I asked.

"Everything God makes is real," she replied. She was quiet for a moment; then continued, "Even if you can't see it, it's real."

She marked the place in her book and closed it gently, and she leaned against me. She held my hand.

"Where I am, it doesn't hurt anymore," she said. "I'm just waiting."

"I know," I whispered.

"Don't feel bad, please," she pleaded softly as she tightened her grip on my hand. "It's okay."

"Maybe I should be telling you that," I said.

She put her head against my shoulder. She felt warm, she felt real; she should be alive.

"How did it happen?" I asked.

"I'll tell you," she said, "but not now. I still have things I have to do. And I want to make sure you're okay before I tell you."

"Make sure I'm okay?" I cried incredulously. "I'm not . . ."

"Dead. No, I'm alive," she said. "I'm just alive in a different way than you and everyone else here is." She smiled, and it comforted me a little.

"I've been watching you," she continued. "You paint beautiful pictures. And you have a lovely oak tree in your backyard. I was there with you that night. I've been watching over you. You kept coming back to me, and the first time I saw you, I knew you had a good heart. I knew you would be the one who wouldn't leave me alone. I knew you would be the one who would set me free. It's all happened so fast."

"Never," I said. "I would never leave you alone."

"I'm always here," she replied. "But unless it's you that comes here, I hide. I know you won't leave me alone; that's why you're here with me now. God has His reasons. We just need to trust Him."

I nodded. "What about your parents?" I asked. "How were they when they found out what happened to you?"

"They had accepted I was gone," she answered. "But when they found out why, they were sad. But I visited them in the same way I visited you, inside your dreams, deep inside your heart. And they know that you're with me, and they know that I'm not alone. They liked that I was with you. My mother is writing you a letter—she thought it would be more personal than this e-mail thing everyone does now. She wants to say thank you.

That's why I'm so glad you gave me your phone number. I left it on their nightstand. And they found your number in the phonebook and then your address."

"I'm so unsure … I don't know what I'm doing."

She put her hand on the back of my head. "You do," she reassured me. "You just don't know it yet."

"If not now," I said, "then when? And if not when, then will it ever?"

"It will make sense, I promise," she said. "You just have to trust me for now."

The sun sank away from us a few hours later.

Chapter Seventeen

I visited her every single day. And we talked, and we walked along the shore and she told me about growing up, and what school was like and how she had taught herself to play the guitar and how she loved to write poetry and take pictures.

And one Saturday morning in late April, she took me by the hands and we stood on the beach and she told me that she was ready to show me what had happened. She put her head against my chest and put her hand up to my heart and she closed her eyes, and the sky covered us in darkness and the stars shot past us and there were brilliant moments of illumination and an array of reds and yellows in an autumn-colored sunset; the leaves on the ground behind us returned to life and fell upwards back onto the trees, and disappeared into preexistence and the years retraced their steps.

The shoreline grew and retreated and as the waves moved relentlessly on in their eternal struggle against the land. The ships and planes ran back and forth; the spring flowers bloomed and faded and bloomed again and the grass grew and then was blanketed by snow and we were caught in a rainstorm but we didn't soak.

The road beyond the little meadow was unpaved now and there were cars that appeared and disappeared and Julia squeezed my hand a little.

And how many thousand days had been remembered? How many countless storms and snowfalls and springs had come and gone and come back? The sun had returned to everything it had once left for eternity; and here we were, somewhere between the past and the present and the future, with everything that had been forgotten but there was a sense of everything that had not yet been realized as well.

The land slipped away and raced past us, and we were on the southern shore of the Island, perhaps on Fire Island, and Julia opened her eyes and the stars were over us and we stood somewhere in the dunes looking out across the beach, at families and playing children and the twinkling reflections of boats and their lights out on the ocean. The trees were dark and full and then out across the water came the tremendous sight of flashes, of fireworks far out over the ocean, and there was cheering, and there were American flags planted into the sand.

And Julia took my hand and we walked down onto the beach. "No one can see us unless I want them to," she said; "And I don't want them to. It's you, and it's me."

And we came before a particular family: a father, a mother, and three children, and perhaps some friends and relatives. One of the three children, a girl, sat on the edge of a blanket between everyone: her eyes were trained on the sky. "I was six," Julia explained. "It's the earliest, happiest memory I have. And I wanted to share it with you."

And the small girl looked over at us, perhaps past us, and smiled. "I knew I would be back here one day," Julia said. "I didn't know why I looked over this way all those years ago, but I do now."

"Let's watch the rest of the fireworks from the dunes," she suggested. "It's quieter there. And I want to remember this night again, and I don't want to forget it. And I wanted you to share this with me, before we go back."

She smiled, as she led me back to the dunes.

Chapter Eighteen

"Where from here?" I asked as fathers picked up sleeping children and mothers packed up blankets and chairs and began heading back to parked cars. Julia closed her eyes and put her hand against my head and the world rushed by us again, and we stood before Julia's high school.

"I'm a little embarrassed," she said. "But I'm over there, over by the steps with some of my friends." I looked over towards a cement wall that ran up alongside the steps to a thin girl, hair in a ponytail, and large glasses across her eyes. Julia buried her head into my chest. "I can't believe that was me." She let out a little laugh.

"I would have done anything if anyone had looked at me the way you do," she said. "I would have done anything if anyone had looked at me at all."

I wrapped her up in my arms and the world rushed by; and then it was night and there were lights on in the school and girls in dresses and guys in suits were sitting on the steps and going into and coming out of the doors.

"Spring in my junior year," said Julia. "Some of the football players thought it would be funny for one of them to ask me to the dance and not show up. I waited there until the dance was over, and I cried myself to sleep for weeks after that. I was heartbroken. I had spent my entire time at high school hoping someone, anyone, would notice me. But no one was ever good enough, until you."

Time ran around us again, and it was autumn the following year. "There I am," said Julia as she pointed down the sidewalk. "By my senior year, I had gotten rid of the glasses, and I had filled out in certain places, and then boys began to notice me. And they noticed me for the wrong reasons."

We were inside the school, in the hallway, and Julia showed me herself at her locker. And she was approached by one of the boys in the yearbook. I went to run over to say something, to stop them, but Julia grabbed me and wrapped her arms around me. "There's nothing you can do," she said. "This is all memory. But you can hold me now."

"I can't imagine how badly you must want to stop this," I said. "That's him, isn't it?"

"Yes," said Julia. "One of them."

I tightened my arms around Julia, and she cuddled up against me even closer.

Weeks passed us by, and Julia repeatedly rejected the advances made by the football player. And she consented, finally, to a movie so that the football player would leave her alone. And then we were in front of Julia's house, and she wouldn't kiss the football player goodnight. But they went out again the next weekend. And then they kissed. I cringed, but Julia held onto me even tighter.

The Fall fell away into the winter, to bitter winds and cold air and gray skies. And by then, Julia was regularly seeing the kid. I watched her and her family go away for Easter, and I watched them come back, and then the world rushed past us and we saw Julia, the football player, and a group of his friends traversing the woods at Eaton's Neck, which were larger back then.

"We were looking for a cemetery," Julia told me. "But we couldn't find it. And we ended up accidentally wandering across someone's property."

We were in Julia's bedroom then, and she was pulling down her shirt and yelling for the kid to get out. "He wanted to go further," she said, "and I wasn't ready. I made sure he knew it.

"And that was when things fell out of my control."

Chapter Nineteen

"He apologized to me at school," Julia continued "And after a week had gone by, I forgave him. He said he had been stressed; he said he had been scouted by colleges and had a bright future ahead of him. And we started seeing each other again under the condition that I establish boundaries, and that he respect those boundaries. He was what I thought I wanted, so I let him back in."

Suddenly we were on the shore, where we always were. "We're not back yet," she said. "Look."

And the blue pickup truck came down the road as Henry Grier drove past it. The truck pulled over, another car pulled up behind it, and Julia, the football player, another girl, and the rest of his friends got out. The sky overhead was darkening quickly.

"Storm," Julia reminisced. "We wanted to watch it come in before the Neck was evacuated, so we came up all the way from the south shore."

I watched as they all walked out to the beach, and then I saw Julia and the football player separate from the others. They wandered off back towards the road, and then across and into the woods; I wanted to follow, I tried to move, but then the world rushed past us and Julia and I stood on the rock ledge over herself and her boyfriend. And they kissed, and then he slid his hand under her shirt and she pushed him. He grabbed her wrist and held her and they struggled against each other and he threw her down. She hit her head and neck on one of the rocks and crumpled up. I tried to move again but Julia held onto me and buried her face in my neck. "I don't want to see this," she whispered.

I saw the kid panic. He stepped back and his hands went up to his hair and he looked around in all directions. And then he ran back out of the woods and I wanted to go after him, to chase him down, to stop him, but Julia wouldn't let me move. I looked at her body, her shaking body, and I noticed for the first time that the scarf she wore was not always crimson. It had once been white.

Ten minutes later, the football player and his friends came back with the boat. It took all of them to carry it, and they could barely manage it. They ended up dropping it across her ribs, then shoving it across her. They covered her up and then buried the boat in leaves and kicked up dirt around it and they left.

And I heard Julia scream from under the boat, and I heard her crying, and I heard the chilling screech of her school ring on the metal bands inside the hull. And Julia started shaking in my arms and her legs gave out and she fell into my lap and I kept her locked up in my arms and held her and she cried. I closed my eyes, and I kissed the top of her head.

When I looked up, we were on the shore again. Julia had fallen asleep against me; her fingers were interwoven with mine.

Chapter Twenty

"Gerald Folger," said Harrison. "Football player and murderer."

I was quiet and Harrison looked up at me from the chair behind his desk. He clasped his hands together and put them up to his chin.

"This is all beyond circumstantial," he argued. "You presented the case clear enough, but I know you know there isn't any hard evidence except a few twenty-year old reports."

"I know,"

"We can't arrest him. We can't do anything."

"Yes, I know," I agreed.

"Then why did you do it?"

"To prove it to myself," I answered.

"Understood." Harrison stretched. "Don't forget. Bowling is moved up an hour this week."

I nodded, and left his office.

Back at my desk I started piling up all the folders and papers again. I breathed in deeply; it was over. Justice, to a marginal degree, had been done. I figured I would send an anonymous letter to Folger at some point over the next week, mailed from somewhere out on the east end; the letter would simply describe what had happened. He would have to spend the rest of his life looking over his shoulder, more than he may have already been doing.

That was all I could do. It was all and I hoped it would be enough for Julia to move on.

And then I wondered how it would be with her gone. When I was with her, she filled a place in my heart that had been empty since I could remember. Something had changed inside me; it was her. I would miss her.

Chapter Twenty-one

"You always come out here when you can't sleep." I thought about her words; they seemed to envelop me the way the wind did. They were words, they existed ethereally; they moved me physically; I shivered. Was she here now? Was she here and I couldn't see her? Who else was here tonight?

The moon had hidden itself away behind dark clouds. The wind was determined but the air itself seemed still, as if the past and the present had become intertwined irrevocably; maybe, in the end, they were. The daffodils had bloomed and some of the trees had blossoms. Spring had come.

It was nearly one in the morning. Every so often a car wound its way through the neighborhood; every so often, there was the distant sound of a car door closing; there were voices, muted and weary. I closed my eyes and leaned back against the tree.

I tried not to think of what Julia had shown me; I tried to think of the present, I tried to think of our fingers entwined and her breathing. I tried not to think of the past, tried not to think of what had happened to her, or to anyone that met an end in that way. It was why I did what I did. The pro-life advocates gave a voice to the unborn; I gave a voice to the dead.

There was still more to do; nothing was done.

Julia, however she existed, and however I felt about her, even that didn't seem to confirm the worthiness of what

I was doing. She had changed me; perhaps, in some way she completed me, but she hadn't validated what I was doing.

And what would be vindication?

Seeing her ascend to that blue light? Seeing the pain wiped away from her eyes like the tears that it had caused? Maybe Jesus putting His hand on my shoulder?

I wondered how men had, in the past, gone about their lives and found what it was they were meant for; what it was they were supposed to find. What was I supposed to find? What was I supposed to realize? Maybe I already knew. Maybe all my chances had passed me by. Perhaps I was meant for nothing.

I thought of the hundreds buried in cemeteries that were lost to time; I thought about the thousands of voices silenced and cut short and their stories forgotten. How many thousands of lives had been lost to the relentless approach of time? How many thousands of stories have never been told?

What was my story?

What was my voice?

Who was I?

I thought of the countless old boathouses and docks that dotted the landscape, worn away by the years and waves. I thought of men, a century ago, spending a day constructing a small wharf; I thought of farmers constructing a barn or a rail fence. I thought of the time they had put into making a claim on time, a claim that never lasted. I thought about the way the chipped paint and worn wood and collapsing stables were now; I thought about the docks that tumbled forward into the streams and the ocean, about the small boats that rested on the seafloor. I thought about how time had disregarded everything in its wake.

I would not forget.

Chapter Twenty-two

"I'm still looking," said Julia. She snuggled into her scarf and she looked at me with wide eyes. "At least I have you," she said. She put her head against my shoulder.

"What are you looking for?" I asked.

"I don't want to trouble you. I've already troubled you so much."

"You never trouble me," I protested.

"I hope I don't," she confessed. "I hope that I've been worth the time you've spent on me."

"How could you not be?" I took her hand and wrapped it in both of mine. She smiled.

"I'm sorry. I think too much sometimes, perhaps. You would tell me if I was too much trouble?"

"I could never tell you because you never are."

"Why are you so good to me?" she asked.

"Because someone needs to be. You've seen things no one should ever have to see."

"But I'm glad I see you. I'm glad for whatever time God has given us."

"Is it that God has given us this time, or is it that it's because you haven't found what you've been looking for?"

"God will come for me when I am ready. He has given us this time. I know you, but I'm cold here unless you're here with me. And I know you can't be here all the time, and I can't often go too far away from here."

"And you're still looking?"

"Yes," she replied. "I'm sorry. I know I'm trouble. And please, believe me." She put her hand on my face and turned it away from the ocean. "I know how much work you put into what happened. I can't tell you how much it means to me that you would be willing to risk so much just to send a letter to Gerald. But that's not what I'm looking for. I'm still looking for it."

"I thought that it would set you free," I explained. "I thought I would make you happy and you could leave."

"Oh, I want to leave," she reassured. "You already make me so happy. You've done for me things I never thought I'd know. I know I'm dead, but I can still feel. You've taken care of me. You always have. And as much as I want to leave, I want to stay here too. I will miss you." She smiled. "But I'll always be here. It doesn't make much sense now, but I promise you that it will."

"Well what can I do?" I asked. "What can I do to help you?" It was a half-truth; I wanted to help her, but I wasn't sure if I was so ready for her to leave.

"You've already done so much,"

'What is it you're looking for?"

I wondered, perhaps, if she was as reluctant to tell me as I was reluctant to hear what it was she had to find. She was quiet; she breathed in deeply and her fingers tightened around mine. She closed her eyes and opened them, as if to steady herself, to reassure herself that she could tell me.

"It's been so long," she whispered.

The sun was a bright orange globe falling away west of us. The sky overhead turned a shade of rose and the edges of red clouds were illuminated as they drifted by. Boats out on the Sound were silhouettes and seagulls dashed above our heads. There were warm gusts of wind amid the cold air.

She took off her gloves and her hands were scraped and torn and bruised; she lifted her fingers up to my lips and touched them. She looked into my eyes and looked back away, and looked at me again. She lifted up her hand so I could see it.

"I lost it when I was under the boat, and I cried. And then there was silence. I woke up, and I cried; it was still gone."

Her ring.

Chapter Twenty-three

"I need to get into the evidence room," I told Harrison the moment he arrived the next morning.

"What for?" he asked.

"I need to go over some of the evidence. I think there was something I may have missed," I lied.

"I would let you. And you know, I don't care. As long as you're doing something productive; but everything has been packed up to be shipped to county storage."

"You shipped it?" I said a little louder than I'd wanted.

"No," he answered. "It's going Monday morning."

"Can I unpack it?"

"No! You know the procedure. If you want to examine it then you're going to have to go through a mountain of paperwork and go look at it at the archives. And then there's the waiting period."

"Why didn't you tell me you were closing the case down?" I said.

"Because nothing came of it. You got what you wanted."

'There was one more thing."

"Well don't worry about it. You've done more than I thought possible with it. After all, it's just another cold case."

No, I thought, she's not just another; she's alive.

He must have seen the indignant impetuousness in my eyes; he sat back in his chair and assumed an air of authority I had never seen him take with me.

"You're a good friend," he said. "That's why I'm telling you not to mess yourself up here. You're already too involved in this thing."

I was quiet. He steepled his fingers.

"Robert, let it go. It's almost summer. And then we're going to have our hands full with more important things. I don't want to have to tell you to take some time off; I've never had to be pushy with you, and I sure don't want to start now."

"I know," I said. "I just—"

"I don't want to hear about it again—not unless you have substantial evidence, not circumstantial."

"Alright," I promised.

"Don't forget," Harrison called after me, "bowling is moved up an hour this Friday."

Chapter Twenty-four

"I can't believe I'm hearing this," Jenson said. He threw his hands up in the air. "At the very least, you're going to be fired."

"I don't care," I persisted. "I know what I have to do."

"Yeah, you're going to get in serious trouble. Why would you do something so stupid?"

"I don't want to make her have to wait," I said. "She's waited too long already."

"Can you find a way that might not end up with you in jail?" Jenson raised an eyebrow. "I'm not going to talk you out of this, am I?"

"No," I admitted. "But thank you for your concern."

"Look, I'm not going to stop trying. Eventually I'll knock some sense into your head. Or I'll have to knock you out."

"I don't have that kind of time."

"You're insane, Robert."

"I probably am," I agreed..

I left Jenson standing at his car and I headed over to mine. I would come back later that night; there would only be two officers on duty at the station. One would be at the front desk, the other in the back. There would be two other officers out on patrol. I didn't go out with everyone that night.

I went home and I read a little. I thought about painting but I didn't seem to have the heart for it. The trees were starting to turn green and soon it would be summer. I wondered if I would ever have the heart to paint on the shore again after everything I had found there.

The sun disappeared sometime. Whenever it slipped into yesterday I wasn't sure. I was too concerned with the future after being consumed for so long by the past.

I pulled up in front of the station a little after midnight. Parker and Emerson were on duty that night. They were both playing poker at the front desk and I waved and mentioned something about forgetting a book and they went back to their game.

I unlocked the door to the evidence room and found the packages of the evidence from Julia's case on a table set against the wall. I pulled out my keys and some packing tape from a nearby shelf; I cut open the first of three boxes and found only files. I cut open the second and found the shreds of her clothing. I cut open the last of the boxes and sorted through some old wood pieces from the boat and pulled out the bag with Julia's ring in it.

I heard a loud bang from outside and I ripped the bag open and put the ring in my pocket. I threw the bag back into the box and crept back over to the door and peered through the narrow window in it. Parker was setting a coat rack back up. I watched him grab a cup of coffee and head back out front, and then I slipped out and shut the door and locked it. I grabbed the book I had purposely left on my desk earlier that day and headed out into the front where I came face-to-face with Harrison.

"You missed bowling," he said.

"I know," I said. I tried to control my breathing. "I wasn't feeling well and so I skipped it."

"What are you doing back here?" he asked. "I mean, if you're not feeling well?"

I held up the book—Leroux's *Phantom of the Opera*—and said as convincingly as I could, "Forgot this. I wanted to finish it."

"Oh," Harrison raised an eyebrow. "I never was into reading. Well we missed you tonight. I'll see you Monday and don't think we'll take it easy on you next weekend."

"I wouldn't think so," I said. I shifted my weight from one foot to the other. "Well, have a good night."

"Take it easy, Rob," he responded. "See you Monday."

I went outside and I breathed in deeply. That had been too close. And then I remembered that the boxes hadn't been re-taped.

Could I go back in? Make some excuse? Come in the next morning earlier than anyone else? I stood there, frozen underneath the parking lot lampposts; my heart was urging me on but the rest of me was telling me to go back, to cover up what I had done. I took a step forward and hesitated, turned back towards the station, turned back towards my car, and headed over to it. As I opened the door I heard Harrison's voice.

"Robert! Don't move! We need to talk! I was just in the evidence room!"

I slammed the door and started the car and swerved out onto the road towards Eaton's Neck.

I had to hurry. I knew Harrison would be following me.

Chapter Twenty-Five

As I pulled onto Pond Drive and raced through and out of patches of woods, I was wondering what would happen to me when Harrison caught up. Whatever would happen, it didn't seem to matter to me. I pulled over off of the road and parked as far into the woods as I could; I hoped that it might buy me some time.

I sprinted through the woods and the darkness was a blur past me. I was heading towards where we had found her. And up ahead through the trees there was light.

I found Julia sitting where she had died, surrounded by a soft, luminescent blue. She was at the center of it, radiating light. She looked so beautiful and her hair was arrayed around her shoulders. Around her there were white flowers and she reached out and touched the ground and beams of light lifted up from the earth and in their place came more flowers; she stood, and as she stood she put out her hand and touched the trunk of a tree and the tree came to life.

She looked at me, and she took steps towards me and she smiled and in her footsteps the forest floor grew and there were white and yellow wildflowers. She wrapped her arms around me and I held onto her as tightly as I could. She was warm and she put her hand on my neck she looked into my eyes and brushed her thumb across my lower lip. Every touch of her skin against mine was like electricity; I was warm for the first time in years and she brought pieces of me to life that I had thought dead and buried.

"I knew you would come tonight," she said.

"You're beautiful," I said.

"No one's ever told me that like you have," she said with a smile. "You always take care of me."

"I have your ring," I told her.

"I know," she replied. "But before I have it, can we look at the ocean one more time?"

"Yes," I said as I bit back a tear; "Of course."

She took me by the hand and she led me out of the dark. It seemed like we drifted across the road and through the meadow and onto the shore. And where we stood existed somewhere between time and eternity, between Heaven and Earth.

"I'm going to miss you so much," said Julia.

"You have no idea how much I'm going to miss you," I answered. "You know, you always tell me that I found you. But I think that you found me."

"Maybe," she said. "But I do know that you found me. And you saved me."

"How?" I asked. "What have I done?"

"More than words could possibly say," She put her head against my shoulder. "I almost don't want to leave."

"It'll be a long time before I see you again,"

She smiled and she looked into my eyes. "No," she said softly. "It'll be as though I'm taking just another step."

"I don't understand," I said. She took both of my hands.

"When I get to Heaven," she explained, "you'll already be there. Time doesn't exist where God is. We're already both together in Heaven. There will be a wait for you, because you're here, and you're in this place. But for me, it'll be like I close my eyes and open them, and you'll already be there holding my hand.

"It's like everyone goes to sleep at different times, but everyone wakes up together."

A tear trickled down her soft face.

"And there is one more thing I have to tell you," she said. "Something you need to know."

"What is it?" I asked.

"Your father wanted me to tell you something."

I couldn't breathe.

"That night, when he was killed . . . it wasn't your fault." I found myself unsure and hesitant to hear what she was telling me. "It wasn't your fault. You were going to the store on the corner to get orange juice for the morning. And you went back inside because you forgot to bring out the keys. And while you were inside, someone came and took your father."

I almost started crying.

"And then you came outside, and you found him. You were eight years old. And you reached down and you touched him and he was quiet and you asked him to wake up but he wouldn't. He couldn't. And for all this time you thought things could be different; that, if you were outside, maybe it wouldn't have happened or you could have saved him somehow.

"But it couldn't have been any different." She put her arms around me and I felt the ground give way beneath me but she caught me.

"He wanted me to tell you that it wasn't your fault. He wanted me to tell you that your mother and brother are with him too. They came here to ask me to talk to you. And you're already with them up there, but for now, in this place, you had to know so you could live your life.

"If you had been out there, you would be dead too. But you're not. You're alive. And you saved me, and you've done so much. But you still have more to do before you can go to sleep and wake up forever."

She held me close to her. I could hear the gentle sweep of the ocean; the wind swirled around us and I felt her start to shake. I looked up and she was crying too.

"The hardest part," she said as she wiped away my tears, "is that I can't take you with me. And it's not that I won't see you as soon as I leave, it's that you'll still be here. I don't have to leave."

I put my hand on her face and she kissed my palm; "It's time to go," I said. "You've been waiting too long. It's time to go see God."

Chapter Twenty-six

She put her forehead against mine and I closed my eyes. Everything we ever have is ripped away; but is it that it is ripped away or that we can't let go? We'll still be here no matter what changes, but this isn't the end, as much as it seems like it is.

And our time will pass us by. And we'll forget. And others will forget. And eventually time will forget. And the broken-down relics of our history will disappear as the years race past, and memories will linger for a while. But we'll all be gone. And someone will uncover a part of our story somewhere.

And although this place may forget us, Jesus never does.

I pulled her ring out of my pocket and I held it out in my hand as I heard car engines up on the road.

She smiled so beautifully when I held it out. She leapt onto me and put her arms around my neck. "Thank you so much," she said. "Thank you so much."

I held it out for her, but she didn't take it right away.

"I always dreamed of getting married," she said. "And when I got my graduation ring, I would pretend that it was my wedding ring. It meant so much to me."
I could hear voices now, far off behind us.

"It's time to go," I said.

"I know."

She reached forward and pulled my neck down and she kissed my lips.

I took her hand and I slipped the ring onto her finger. "I'll see you soon," I said.

"Harrison! Stop!"

We both looked over to the edge of the sand and Jenson was chasing Harrison, who was sprinting towards us.

"Thank you," she said, "for everything. I love you." She put a small, folded piece of paper into my pocket.

But she didn't give me a chance to respond. She already knew.

She kissed me again and she stepped backwards as Jenson and Harrison slowed to a walk. The blue light that surrounded her grew stronger, and she waved and turned towards the ocean. She stepped into the water and as she did, the ocean lit up with each step she took and light coursed away from her in all directions. The wind picked up and Julia's hair swirled in the air. She turned around one last time, and she was glowing white now. She reached down and touched the waves with her fingertips and light radiated away from her back to the shore.

Overhead, in the darkness there came a great blue light and it seemed to part the sky. From it came great streaks of sky blue light and they fell around Julia.

She reached up her arms and the lights transformed into one solid beam. Everything was light and then she was lifted up out of the water; all of the light that had poured out from her returned to her as she drifted up and away.

I watched her rise into the sky and I wiped away my tears. And then as suddenly as she had come into my life, she was gone. The light disappeared from the sky and everything was quiet and dark.

And I felt so bitterly alone and I managed to stop myself from crying. I knew I would later, but for now, I couldn't. It felt as though everything inside of me was gone and taken away. And I thought, no, it's not that you're taken away. It's that we're still left here to miss what's gone. And it'll only be a matter of time before we go to sleep too.

And wake up together.

I felt a hand on my shoulder; it was Jenson. "I'm still here," he said.

"I know," I answered quietly. "I know."

"So… Harrison remarked as he stepped up beside us, "I think someone needs to tell me I'm not hallucinating."

"No," I replied. "I took her ring."

"I know," Harrison acknowledged.. "I don't care. Not after that. Jenson got here right before I did, and he tried to tell me everything before I came over here. If I didn't see it, I doubt I would have believed it."

"Thomas too," I spoke as I thought about Jesus.

"I'll see you at the station tomorrow," said Harrison. "We have some repacking to do and a packing list to retype. And then Monday I'm sending you and Jenson out to investigate a robbery. I've had more than enough of putting you two on homicides for the time being."

Jenson laughed and I smiled as best I could. "I'll see you tomorrow."

Harrison and Jenson turned to walk back to their cars.

"And by the way," I added as they turned around for a moment. "Thank you. Both of you."

Harrison nodded and Jenson waved. "Just don't skip next Friday," Jenson added as a reminder..

I waved as they went away. I walked over to the edge of the water and I looked up.

"Good night," I whispered into the wind. I knew Julia would hear me.

When I got home, I sat down on my couch and looked over to my wall where I had photos of my family. I got up, and I walked into my little studio, and came out with the sketch I had made of Julia and one of her photographs. I put them up on the wall; I would get frames for them tomorrow after I left the station.

When I got ready for bed, I remembered the paper Julia had put into my pocket. I pulled it out, and unfolded it, and across it in her flowing handwriting was a small poem, and a little note she had written to me:

And every so often
Should the soul, condemned to wander
Retracing footsteps long since faded,
Meet upon the present age
The memories reawakened
Will close one story
And begin another
And there will be a time
A place
When we will be together
When the world has passed us by
And we will wake up in each others arms

Robert,
You'll never know how much this meant to me; how much you mean to me.
Don't be sad. I'll always be right there with you. You're already here with me.
Everything will be okay, I promise.

Everything will be okay.

I love you.
-Julia

...from eternity to eternity you are God.
A thousand years in your eyes is merely a yesterday...
Psalms 90:2-4

ABOUT THE AUTHOR

Joe Vigliotti, a writer and artist, resides in Maryland. He is a graduate of Mount Saint Mary's University, where he studied history, philosophy, and political science. Through his work, he strives to capture some essence of God's meaning for humanity.

Other FutureWord books by Joe Vigliotti:

Carnival Week

www.ingramcontent.com/pod-product-compliance
Lightning Source LLC
Chambersburg PA
CBHW020630130626
46552CB00003B/1154